The Boy In The Drawer

Story • Robert Munsch

Art • Michael Martchenko

©1986 Bob Munsch Enterprises Ltd. (Revised edition, text)
©1986 Michael Martchenko (art)
Twenty-fifth printing, May 2007

Annick Press Ltd.

We acknowledge the support of the Canada Council for the Arts, the Ontario Arts
Council, and the Government of Canada through the Book Publishing Industry
Development Program (BPIDP) for our publishing activities.

Cataloging in Publication Data
  Munsch, Robert N., 1945-
    The boy in the drawer

  (Munsch for kids)
  ISBN 0-920236-34-0 (bound) ISBN 0-920236-36-7 (pbk.)

  I. Martchenko, Michael. II. Title. III. Series:
  Munsch, Robert N., 1945- Munsch for kids.

  PS8576.U58B69   jC813'.54   C82-094155-7
  PZ7.M86Bo

Distributed in Canada by:	Published in the U.S.A. by Annick Press (U.S.) Ltd.
Firefly Books Ltd.	Distributed in the U.S.A. by:
66 Leek Crescent	Firefly Books (U.S.) Inc.
Richmond Hill, ON	P.O. Box 1338, Ellicott Station
L4B 1H1	Buffalo, NY 14205

Printed and bound in China.

visit us at: **www.annickpress.com**

Annick Press Ltd.
Toronto • New York • Vancouver

When Shelley went into her room, there were socks on the floor, socks on the bed, socks on the dresser, socks on the wall, and socks everywhere. "Yikes!" said Shelley. "What a mess."

And from out of the sock drawer somebody yelled, "BE QUIET."

So Shelley crawled across the floor and very carefully looked into the drawer. A small boy was sitting there reading a book.

Shelley ran downstairs and said, "Mommy, Mommy, there is a boy in my sock drawer."

"Tell him to go home," said the mother.

"And there are socks all over my room."

"Clean them up," said the mother.

"But, but, but ..."

"Clean them up," said the mother.

So Shelley went back upstairs and looked in the drawer. The boy was gone. She cleaned up the whole room and went downstairs for lunch.

When Shelley went back upstairs, there was a large bump in the middle of the bed. She pulled back the covers and there was the boy, watering a tomato plant.

Shelley ran downstairs and said, "Mommy, Mommy, my bed is a mess."

"Clean it up," said the mother.

"But, but, but ..."

"Clean it up," said the mother.

When Shelley went back upstairs, the boy was gone. She cleaned up the whole mess by herself.

Shelley went downstairs and read a book. The room started to get dark. Shelley looked around and saw a big bump behind the drape. She very quietly crawled over to the drape and yanked it up.

There was the boy. He was painting the window black.

"Go away!" said Shelley. The boy grew five centimeters.

"Beat it," said Shelley. The boy grew five more centimeters.

Shelley took a paintbrush and painted the boy's ear black. He grew five more centimeters.

"Help!" yelled Shelley, and she ran off to find her mother and father.

They weren't in the basement and they weren't upstairs. They were in the kitchen. So was a lot of water. It was all coming out of the breadbox.

Shelley walked very quietly to the breadbox and yanked it open.

There was the boy. He was taking a bath. He said, "Please go away. You are bothering me."

Shelley had an idea. She turned the hot water all the way off, and she turned the cold water all the way on. When the cold water hit the boy, he jumped up, grew 50 centimeters, and sat in the middle of the kitchen table.

The father and mother both said, "Shelley, tell your friend to go home."

So Shelley said, "Beat it."

The boy grew 10 centimeters.

Shelley decided to try something different. Very carefully, she walked over and patted the boy. Right away, he got a little smaller. Then her father went to the table and gave the boy a hug. He got very small.

Then her mother gave the boy a kiss, and he disappeared entirely.

"And who will clean up the kitchen?" said the mother.

"And who will clean up the kitchen?" said the father.

"And who will clean up the kitchen?" said Shelley.

And the mother gave Shelley a hug.

And the father gave Shelley a hug.

And she cleaned up the whole mess with no trouble at all.